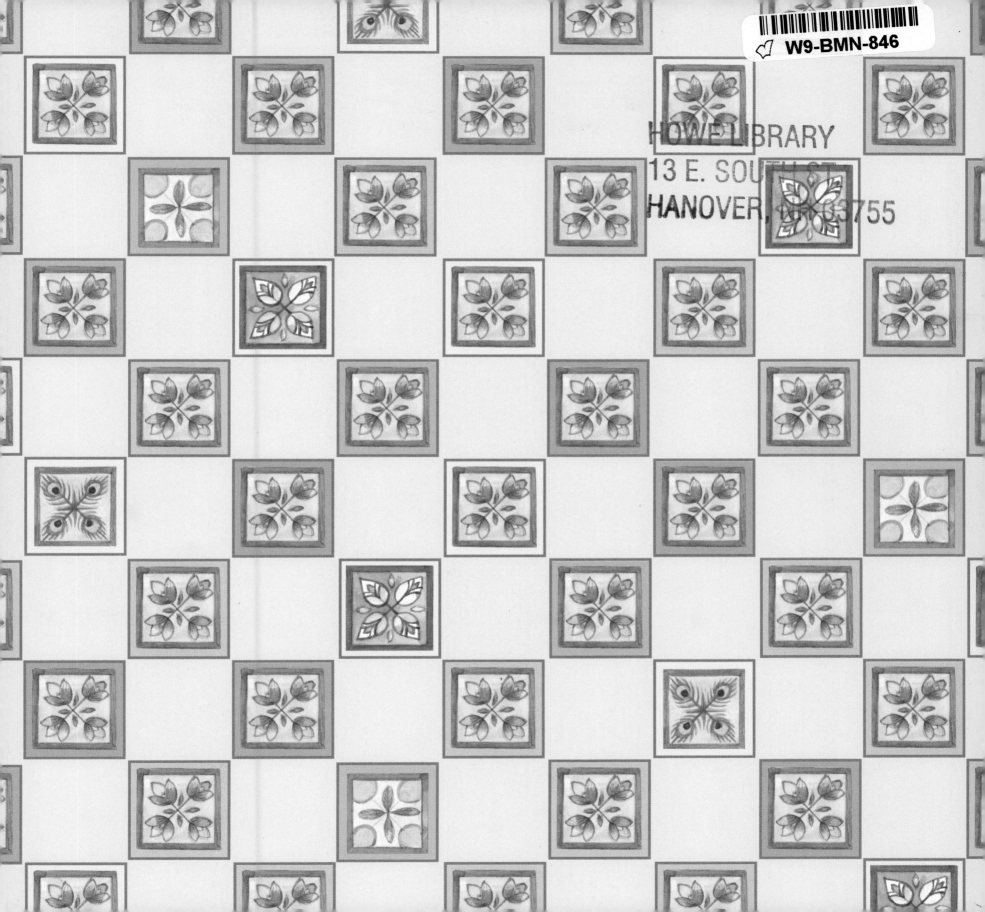

Monsoon Afternoon

For Rajan
—*K. S.*

To Pierre and Grandpa Jaeggi
—*Y. J.*

Published by
PEACHTREE PUBLISHERS
1700 Chattahoochee Avenue
Atlanta, Georgia 30318-2112
www.peachtree-online.com

Text © 2008 by Kashmira Sheth
Illustrations © 2008 by Yoshiko Jaeggi

Book and cover design by Yoshiko Jaeggi and Loraine M. Joyner
Illustrations created in watercolor on 100% rag, hot press archival watercolor paper; text typeset in Adobe's Sabon, title typeset in Monotype Imaging's Calisto with Samual Wang's Harrington initial capitals. Author's note typeset in International Typeface Corporation's Stone Sans and Harrington.

Printed in China
10 9 8 7 6 5 4 3 2 1

Library of Congress Cataloging-in-Publication Data

Sheth, Kashmira.
   Monsoon afternoon / written by Kashmira Sheth ; illustrated by Yoshiko Jaeggi. -- 1st ed.
      p. cm.
   Summary: A young boy and his grandfather find much they can do together on a rainy day during monsoon season in India.
   ISBN 13: 978-1-56145-455-6 / ISBN 10: 1-56145-455-9
   [1. Rain and rainfall--Fiction. 2. Monsoons--Fiction. 3. Grandfathers--Fiction. 4. India--Fiction.]
I. Jaeggi, Yoshiko, ill. II. Title.
   PZ7.S5543Mo 2008
   [E]--dc22
                     2008004565

Monsoon Afternoon

Written by

Kashmira Sheth

Illustrated by

Yoshiko Jaeggi

PEACHTREE
ATLANTA

Outside I saw dark clouds roll like ocean waves across the sky. The temple flag fluttered loudly. The peacocks called out, *tahuoonk, tahuoonk.*

The dogs woke up and stretched their legs, and the cows got up and left.
Ants scurried across the ground as if the earth were one big maze.

I counted the raindrops, one, two, three. Soon there were too many to count. On the patio, the rain fell fast, cutting the heat in half.

"Dadima, can you come out and play?" I asked.

"Not now. I want to drink my tea," she said, going in the kitchen.

I peeked in Mommy's room. "Please, come out and play."
"Not now. My patients are waiting for me at the clinic,"
she said, picking up her umbrella.

"Pappa, will you come out?"

"Not now. I have to finish this story," he said, scribbling in his notepad.

"Jai, let's play," I said to my brother.
"Not now. I'm hungry," he said, picking up one banana and two guavas.

I stuck my face out the door and caught some raindrops on my forehead.

"What are you doing?" asked Dadaji.

"Nothing," I sighed.

"You look as glum as an ink pot. What's the matter?"

"No one wants to go out and play with me."

"Are you sure?" Dadaji's mustache shook slightly, and I saw a smile hiding in it.

The old washtub was almost full of rainwater. "Can we sail boats?" I asked.

"Of course we can," Dadaji said.

We each made three different kinds of boats from paper.

One after the other, we raced our boats until they got wet and soggy and sank to the bottom of the washtub sea.

"It looks like you are wearing pearl earrings," I said to Dadaji. When he shook his head, they fell off, but two new raindrops slid in their places. By now the rain was tired. It sprinkled just one tiny drop after another.

"Let's take a walk, Dadaji," I said.
I looked at the ground and there were no cracks.
"What happened to all the ants?" I asked.
"They are all safe and snug in their homes," Dadaji replied.

We stopped to watch a peacock dancing.

When we drew closer, it silently spread its beautiful tail feathers.

"Look how shiny the leaves of the banyan tree are now," I said, picking up a wet fallen leaf.

"They are," Dadaji said, smiling. "Do you want to swing?"

He lifted me up. I grabbed the roots of the banyan tree and swung back and forth.

Then he lifted me onto his shoulders.

"Dadaji, did you ever swing on this banyan tree?"

"Oh yes. Very often," he said.

I tried to imagine Dadaji swinging on the banyan tree.

I tried to imagine him as small as me, sitting on his dadaji's shoulders.

"Did monsoon come when you were little?" I asked.

"Of course. Monsoon came every year when I was little. Just like it does now."

"Did peacocks dance in the rain and did ants
disappear when you were little?"
Dadaji nodded. "They always did."

"Will monsoon come when I become a dadaji?"
"Yes, it will," Dadaji replied.

We picked the last few mangoes from the mango tree. Dadima opened the door and called, "Come in and put on dry clothes this instant, before you both catch cold!"

Dadaji and I gave Dadima all the mangoes and hurried to our rooms to change.

When we came out, Dadima was standing by the door with her hand on her hip. "Look at the mud you two have tracked in," she scolded. "Who do you think is going to clean this mess?"

"We are," Dadaji and I said together.

I grabbed a rag and Dadaji picked up a pail.
"Did your dadima scold you and make you clean up?" I whispered to Dadaji.
"She sure did," Dadaji answered.

Dadima came back with three steaming cups of tea. The smell
of ginger and cinnamon filled the air.

"What are you two talking about?" she asked.

Dadaji and I scrubbed the floor extra hard.
"Nothing," we replied. "Nothing at all."

A Note from the Author

I GREW UP on the west coast of India.
When summer heat became unbearable, there was only one
thing to do: wait for monsoon to bring rain and relief. The moist
wind blew in from the Arabian Ocean, the dark clouds swirled,
and then the heavens opened up. All the children in my family
would run to the open courtyard and catch the raindrops on our
tongues, make paper boats to sail in puddles of water, and chase
each other as the rain soaked us. We'd sing a rhyme in Gujarati:

> *Come rain, (you're) a gift from the heaven.*
> *(Time for) warm roti and bitter squash.*

Even though I didn't like bitter squash, I sang
with great enthusiasm because the rain meant
the end of the dusty, brown, hot summer.
The monsoon washed away the dust from
the windowsills, painted the earth green, and
filled the dry riverbeds. In a matter of days,
vines sprouted and climbed up the banyan
trees, fields turned lush, and water pumps
stood abandoned.

We had a huge jamboo tree in one corner of our yard, and
every monsoon it was covered with purple fruit. I loved the
sweet, juicy jamboos that tasted like miniature plums. Once
the rains came, we children were not allowed to eat snow cones

or other foods from street vendors because of the risk of diseases like cholera, typhoid, and dysentery. Every morning, my grandmother gave us juice of neem leaves to prevent sickness. The juice was so bitter that even a glass of milk couldn't wash the taste away.

Monsoon arrived in Western India around the second week of June. It was also the time when the new school year began, so along with a shiny raincoat and squeaky new gumboots, it was time to buy books, pencils, and notebooks.

If the rain was especially heavy, school was cancelled. We played cards and board games at home and watched the sheets of water coming down. Sometimes, storms raged with scary lightning, thunder, and nasty winds. The streets flooded and turned into rivers. In certain areas of the country, entire villages were swept away by the torrential rains.

Rim-zim…rim-zim. The rain made music when it was soft and gentle. Sometimes, when the winds blew very hard, it was almost impossible for the people on the street to hold on to their umbrellas, which were usually black. The wind turned them inside out, making the umbrellas look like big black crows. Whenever that happened, we children pointed and shouted, "Umbrella crow! Umbrella crow!"

Monsoon also brought the end of mango season, because after the rains the mangoes turned soft and rotted quickly. We had to wait another eight or nine months for our favorite fruit. We didn't mind. Year after year, we welcomed the rainy season because it marked a new cycle of growth, like spring in my current home, Wisconsin.

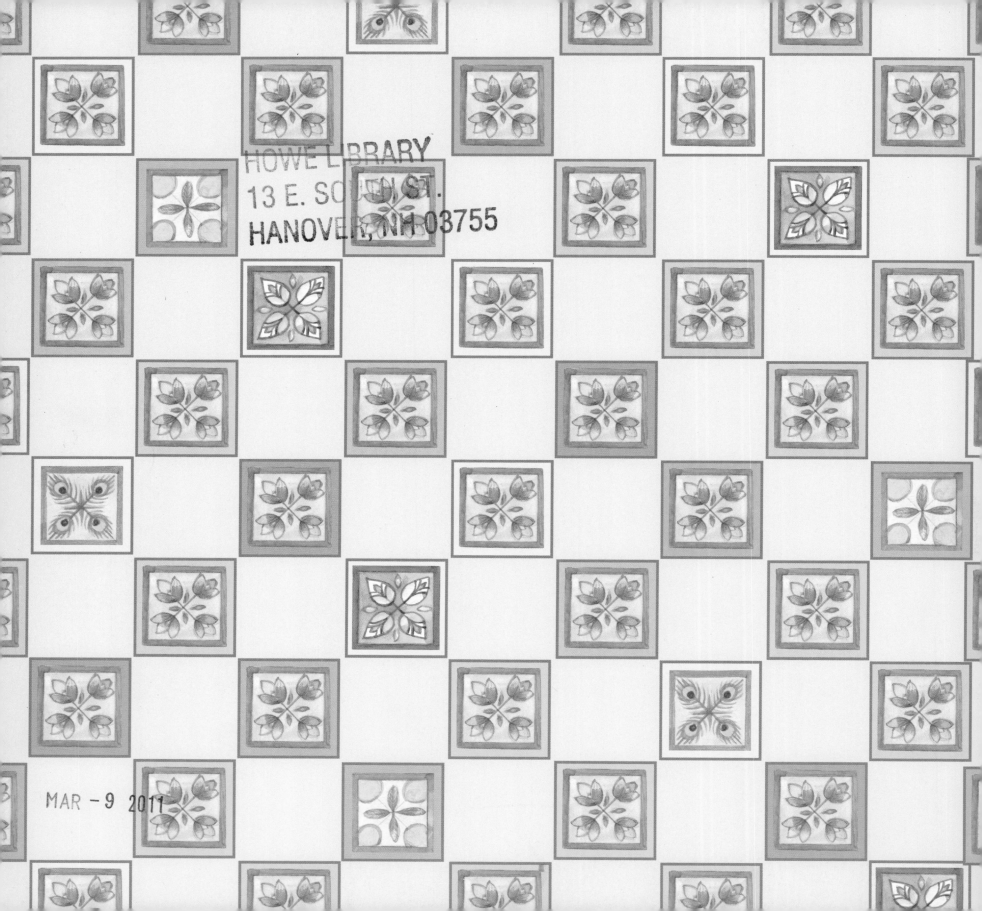